And J.J. Slept

To Mom, for filling our home with so much. To Jim and the loving families he found. — L.G.

For Lalo and for my other caring friends who are always there for me — E.M.

Published in Canada and the U.S. by Kids Can Press Ltd.
25 Dockside Drive, Toronto, ON M5A 0B5

Kids Can Press is a Corus Entertainment Inc. company

www.kidscanpress.com

The artwork in this book was rendered digitally in Photoshop and Procreate.
The text is set in Colby.

Edited by Katie Scott
Designed by Michael Reis

Printed and bound in Buji, Shenzhen, China, in 10/2021 by WKT Company

CM 22 0 9 8 7 6 5 4 3 2 1

FSC
www.fsc.org
MIX
Paper from
responsible sources
FSC® C010256

Library and Archives Canada Cataloguing in Publication

Title: And J.J. slept / written by Loretta Garbutt ; illustrated by Erika Rodriguez Medina.
Names: Garbutt, Loretta, 1961– author. | Medina, Erika, illustrator.
Identifiers: Canadiana 20210196289 | ISBN 9781525304194 (hardcover)
Classification: LCC PS8613.A688 A83 2022 | DDC jC813/.6 — dc23

Kids Can Press gratefully acknowledges that the land on which our office is located is the traditional territory of many nations, including the Mississaugas of the Credit, the Anishnabeg, the Chippewa, the Haudenosaunee and the Wendat peoples, and is now home to many diverse First Nations, Inuit and Métis peoples.

We thank the Government of Ontario, through Ontario Creates; the Ontario Arts Council; the Canada Council for the Arts; and the Government of Canada for supporting our publishing activity.

And J.J. Slept

Written by Loretta Garbutt
Illustrated by Erika Rodriguez Medina

KIDS CAN PRESS

Wrapped in the softness of his blanket, J.J. finally arrived at his new home. His family was bubbling over with excitement to meet him.

The woman from the adoption agency watched as J.J. met his new family for the first time.

"Welcome," said Harvey.

"Hi, little guy," said Ada.

Sebastian squeezed in. "So small."

Etta giggled and touched J.J.'s soft, tiny hand.

Then Harvey sneezed. "Excuse me."
The kettle whistled. "I'll get it," said Ada.
"OW!" screeched Sebastian as Etta stepped
on his toe.

The washing machine beeped, and Cheddar yelped to be let out.
"Try to keep it down, everyone," whispered Dad.

And J.J. slept.

The next morning, the
kids thundered through
the house.

Sebastian drummed
on the kitchen table.

"Where's my inhaler?"
Harvey yelled.

"My costume has a rip," sobbed Etta.

Ada took a barking Cheddar out for his walk.

And J.J. slept.

That first week, J.J. did all sorts of typical baby things.

"Not much seems to bother this little fella," said Dad.
"He sleeps through it all," said Mom.
"And *it all* seems louder than usual," said Dad.

"Coming in for a landing!" Sebastian
hollered to ground control.

"Did you say something?" shouted Harvey.

"I can't find my piano book," called Ada.

Etta chattered on endlessly to Cheddar.

And J.J. slept.

The next weekend, the house was quiet. Too quiet!
   Harvey was out of town for a dance competition.
Ada was learning a piano duet at a sleepover. Sebastian
had hockey camp. And Etta had gone to visit Gramma
and Grampa.
   The washing machine whirred. Cheddar softly
snored. But there were a whole bunch of other sounds
that were missing.

Surrounded by all that silence, J.J. could not sleep.

J.J. fussed. He kicked. He balled up his little fists and waved them in the air.

Dad held him close, fed him and changed his diaper. Mom sang her best version of "Hush, Little Baby."

But still, J.J. would not sleep.

The next day, J.J. was crankier than ever.
Mom and Dad tiptoed in stocking feet and
whispered over coffee about what to do.

They were all out of ideas when
the front door banged open.

"I'm home!" Harvey shuffle-hop-stepped his way inside.

"Listen to my new piece." Ada plunked herself down at the piano.

Etta went on and on about her wagon ride at the apple farm.

CRASH! Sebastian knocked over the potted plant. "Sorry."

And J.J. stopped crying.

Then the washing machine beeped,
the kettle whistled and the kids giggled
as they chased Cheddar around the
dining room table.

J.J. let out a big yawn and closed his eyes.

Everything was just as it should be.
It sounded like home.
And J.J. slept.